Vegetable Soup

Story by Jeanne Modesitt • Pictures by Robin Spowart

Macmillan Publishing Company   New York
Collier Macmillan Publishers   London

Macmillan Publishing Company
866 Third Avenue, New York, NY 10022
Collier Macmillan Canada, Inc.

Printed and bound in Japan
First American Edition
10 9 8 7 6 5 4 3 2 1
The text of this book is set in 13 pt. Candida.
The illustrations are rendered in watercolor.

Library of Congress Cataloging-in-Publication Data
Modesitt, Jeanne. Vegetable soup. Summary: Two rabbits, seeking carrots for the first lunch in their new home and receiving a variety of foods from their animal neighbors, are at first reluctant to sample anything they have never eaten before.
[1. Food habits—Fiction. 2. Neighborliness—Fiction. 3. Rabbits—Fiction. 4. Animals—Fiction] I. Spowart, Robin, ill. II. Title. PZ7.M715Ve 1988 [E] 87-11169
ISBN 0-02-767630-7

To sister Kate,
whom we love madly

Theodore and Elsie were about to have their first lunch in their new home. Elsie had poured some water into a small cooking pot, and Theodore had lit the fire inside the stove. But when Theodore opened the carrot sack, he let out a gasp. "Oh, dear!" he cried. "It's empty. And the market is closed today."

Theodore and Elsie sat down at their kitchen table, wondering what to do. "Perhaps we could borrow some carrots from our neighbors," Elsie finally suggested.

"Splendid idea," said Theodore. And he and his wife put on their Sunday best and went out into their new neighborhood.

 Soon the rabbits arrived at a small, cheerful-looking house. Theodore and Elsie knocked on the door for what seemed a long time. All at once it flew open, and there stood a wide-eyed squirrel with a bucket of rags and a tall broom.

"Good morning," said Elsie. "I hope we didn't disturb you. We're your new neighbors."

"Come, come!" said the squirrel, tapping her broom on the floor. "I haven't time for chatter. There's too much cleaning to be done."

"We were wondering," continued Elsie quickly, "if we could borrow some carrots."

"For our favorite lunch," added Theodore, "boiled carrots."

"Sorry," said the squirrel, wrinkling her nose. "I don't eat anything that grows underground. Too dusty." And with that she stepped outside and began to sweep the garden path furiously.

Suddenly the squirrel stopped. "Dandelion leaves," she said. "And freshly washed this morning. Now, there's a proper lunch for rabbits. Quite a tasty one, too."

The squirrel scurried over to a small cluster of yellow flowers, pulled off a few leaves, and swept her way back to the rabbits.

"Thank you very much," said Elsie, politely accepting the leaves. "You're very kind."

"But we've never eaten dandelion leaves before," said Theodore after the squirrel had said good-bye and sped back into her house. "I don't want something for lunch that I've never eaten before."

"Neither do I," said Elsie. "But there's no need for us to worry. We have many other neighbors to see." And down the road they went.

 The rabbits had walked barely ten minutes, when off to the side of the road they spotted an old, moss-covered oak tree—the kind that's sure to house a neighbor. "Hello!" they shouted. "Is anyone home?"

A blue jay poked his head out from the branches. "Good morning, travelers," he said.

"Perhaps you could help my husband and me," said Elsie. "We're new in the neighborhood, and we would like to borrow some carrots."

"For our favorite lunch," added Theodore, "boiled carrots."

"Carrots?" the blue jay asked. "One moment, please." And he disappeared into the branches.

The blue jay returned with a worn-looking book and began to flip through the pages. "Aha!" he said. "Here we are. Carrots. 'An orange, spindle-shaped root adored for centuries by rabbits.'" He closed the book. "Of course," he said. "Carrots. I'll check my nest and be right back."

The rabbits had to cover their heads as small twigs and dried leaves rained down on them.

"Terribly sorry," shouted the blue jay from inside the branches. "I seem to be out of carrots. But I think you'll enjoy this."

The bird flew down with the book under his wing and something green in his beak. He dropped the green thing into Elsie's basket. "'Parsley,'" he said smartly, reciting from his book. "'A crinkled green plant'"—he paused dramatically—"'belonging to the carrot family.'"

"Thank you very much," said Elsie. "You're very kind."

"But we've never eaten parsley before," said Theodore after the blue jay had bowed his head and sailed back into the tree. "I don't want something for lunch that I've never eaten before."

"Neither do I," said Elsie. "But there's no need for us to worry. We have many other neighbors to see." And down the road they went.

Before long the rabbits came upon a well-shaded patio. There stood a small round table, and at that table sat two equally round toads.

"Good morning, ladies," said Theodore and Elsie.

The toads looked at the rabbits. "Sister, dear," said the elder one, "I believe we have company."

"You're quite right," said the younger toad. Then she turned to her sister. "Isn't this exciting," she said. "A pair of kangaroos have come to tea."

"I beg your pardon," said Elsie stiffly. "My husband and I are your new neighbors. Your new *rabbit* neighbors. And we would like to borrow some carrots."

"For our favorite lunch," said Theodore, "boiled carrots."

"Rabbits?" said the younger toad.

The elder looked embarrassed. "You must forgive my sister and me. We've never had a rabbit—or a kangaroo—in our neighborhood."

 "Nor," added the younger toad, "have we ever been introduced to carrots."

"Do they go well with tea?" asked her sister good-naturedly.

The rabbits let out a long sigh. "Quite well," said Elsie.

The sisters exchanged glances. Then the elder one rose from the table. "Come, dear," she said. "We must not let our guests leave without a sample of our most treasured treat."

"Certainly not," agreed the younger toad. And the sisters strode to a large wooden barrel, pulled out several handfuls of cherry tomatoes, and carried them back to the rabbits.

"Thank you very much," said Elsie. "You're very kind."

"But we've never eaten tomatoes before," said Theodore after the toads had kissed the rabbits' cheeks and strolled back to their table. "I don't want something for lunch that I've never eaten before."

"Neither do I," said Elsie. "But there's no need for us to worry. We have many other neighbors to see." And down the road they went.

 Some time later, the rabbits found themselves at a large vegetable garden. Off to one side, down on his hands and knees, a hedgehog was pulling weeds.

"Good morning," said Elsie.

"I suppose," mumbled the hedgehog as he pulled out another stubborn weed.

"We're your new neighbors," continued Elsie cordially, "and we would like to borrow some carrots."

"For our favorite lunch," added Theodore, "boiled carrots."

The hedgehog looked up at the rabbits in disgust. "Did you say *carrots*?" he asked. "You eat *carrots* for lunch?"

"Yes," replied Elsie. "Boiled carrots. A perfectly delightful lunch."

"Delightful!" the hedgehog cried. "How could something with little green tops that look like weeds be delightful!"

Before Elsie could respond, the hedgehog groaned and stood up stiffly. "Wait here," he said. "I'll bring you something for your lunch. Something that doesn't look, taste, or even smell like a weed. *Nothing* can be more delightful than that." And so saying, he walked to the far corner of his garden, picked up two round, leafy heads of cabbage, and presented them to the rabbits.

"Thank you very much," said Elsie. "You're very kind."

"But we've never eaten cabbage before," said Theodore after the hedgehog had shaken his head and trudged back to his weeds. "I don't want something for lunch that I've never eaten before."

"Neither do I," said Elsie. "But I'm afraid I have some terrible news. It looks as if we have no other neighbors to see."

 Elsie pointed to a sign hanging from a nearby tree: ROAD ENDS HERE.

Theodore blinked at the sign, then looked down at his wife's basket. "Oh, dear," he said, trying to hold back the tears. "I was so looking forward to a hot bowl of boiled carrots for lunch."

Elsie shook her head and sighed. "We had better head home," she said at last, her voice more quiet than usual.

"I suppose so," said Theodore. He wrapped his arm around his wife's, and they began their journey back.

When the rabbits reached home, Elsie emptied her basket onto the kitchen table. Out came the squirrel's sparkling-clean dandelion leaves, the blue jay's delicate parsley, the toads' bright red tomatoes, and the hedgehog's sturdy cabbage heads.

"How pretty everything looks," said Elsie. "What a pity none of it is carrots."

"Quite a pity," agreed Theodore.

Elsie picked up a dandelion leaf and held it before her. "How strange that the squirrel called dandelion leaves tasty."

Theodore ran his fingers through the parsley. "And who would have thought that parsley had such a good reputation."

"Why, I believe the toads said tomatoes were their favorite treat."

"And we saw how the hedgehog loved his cabbage."

 The rabbits sat in silence for a moment. Then Elsie drew in a deep breath and turned to Theodore. "I know we've never eaten these vegetables before," she said hesitantly, "but why don't we throw everything into the big cooking pot and try to make a soup out of it?"

"Why not!" said Theodore, suddenly feeling quite daring.

And so the rabbits cut and shredded and chopped and sliced. One hour later, they dipped two spoons bravely into the cooking pot and brought them slowly to their mouths.

"Why, this is delicious!" said Elsie.

"Indeed it is," nodded Theodore happily.

"The only thing," said Elsie, "that would make it even more delicious is—"

"Company!" cried Theodore.

And Elsie and Theodore went out to invite their new neighbors to lunch. They couldn't wait to share their first vegetable soup.

How to Make

Vegetable Soup

(with a grown-up's help)

• • •

3 to 4 packed cups chopped dandelion leaves
(spinach leaves may be substituted)
½ cup finely chopped parsley
15 to 20 cherry tomatoes, sliced into halves
3 cups shredded green cabbage
4 cups water
⅛ teaspoon pepper
½ teaspoon salt, if desired

In a large pot, put the dandelion (or spinach) leaves, parsley, cherry tomatoes, cabbage, water, pepper, and salt. Bring the soup to a boil, reduce the heat, and cover the pot. Then simmer the soup until vegetables are tender, about 20 to 30 minutes. Makes four to six servings.

• • •